WOOLLY MAMMOTH IN TROUBLE

by Dawn Bentley

Illustrated by Karen Carr

To Alexander David Bentley, the newest member of the Bentley family. I can't wait for the day I get to listen to you read this book. Love, Aunt Dawn—D.B.

To Dale, Alisa, Christopher and Dylan Winkler—K.C.

Published by Soundprints Division of Trudy Corporation, Norwalk, Connecticut.

Book design: Marcin D. Pilchowski
Editor: Laura Gates Galvin

First Edition 2004
10 9 8 7 6 5 4 3 2 1
Printed in China

Acknowledgements:
    Our very special thanks to Dr. Don E. Wilson of the Department of Systematic Biology at the Smithsonian Institution's National Museum of Natural History.
    Soundprints would also like to thank Ellen Nanney and Katie Mann of the Smithsonian Institution for their help in the creation of this book.

Library of Congress Cataloging-in-Publication Data is on file with the publisher and the Library of Congress.

Woolly Mammoth in Trouble

by Dawn Bentley

Illustrated by Karen Carr

 Soundprints
Where Children Discover...

The chilly sky begins to fill with clouds. A storm is coming, but Woolly Mammoth doesn't seem to notice—he is too busy eating plants buried under the snow. As a creature of the Ice Age, he is used to dealing with the constant wintry conditions.

Woolly Mammoth digs his long tusks into the snow to uncover his food. His long trunk has a pointed, finger-like tip at the end that is just right for grabbing the plants he puts in his mouth.

Woolly Mammoth is huge and he needs a lot of food to fill his belly. He eats almost 200 pounds of vegetation a day! It takes a long time to find that much food.

The snow is beginning to fall harder and faster. It is difficult to see anything through the thick sheet of white snow that fills the air.

Woolly Mammoth cannot find his herd. The storm has grown too strong for Woolly Mammoth. He must look for shelter.

Soon, Woolly Mammoth sees a cave that is just big enough for him to stand in. He goes in and waits there until the storm is over.

Finally, only a few scattered snowflakes are falling. The snow-covered land is quiet and still. Woolly Mammoth leaves the cave and continues searching for his herd, eating all the plants he can find along the way.

Woolly Mammoth does not feel safe without the protection of his herd. Now he senses danger is near. He quickly looks up and sees the danger: Three saber-tooth tigers are standing on an icy ledge above.

The saber-tooth tigers lunge at Woolly
Mammoth, trying to tackle him from all
sides. But Woolly Mammoth is much bigger
and stronger than the ferocious cats.

Woolly Mammoth stomps his big hairy feet and points his long tusks and trunk at the saber-tooth tigers. The frightened cats stumble backward and run away. Now Woolly Mammoth can safely continue searching for his herd.

23

Woolly Mammoth smells a familiar scent and looks around, again relying on his keen eyesight to help him. In the distance he sees twelve woolly mammoths slowly walking in a line. He has found his herd!

Woolly Mammoth calls out to get their attention. They hear his signal and stop so he can catch up. Glad to be with his group again, he immediately falls in line and begins walking with them. Together they roam the cold land in search of more food.

ABOUT THE WOOLLY MAMMOTH

Woolly mammoths lived on earth until about 4,000 years ago. People existed during the time of the woolly mammoths. Woolly mammoths were very much like the elephants of today, except they were bigger and had hair. They weighed about 15,000 pounds and were around twelve feet tall!

Woolly mammoths were built for cold weather. Their bodies were covered with a thick layer of fat, an undercoat of fur, and an overcoat of long brown hair. These three layers helped protect them from the freezing temperatures of the Ice Age. Woolly mammoths were herbivores and spent nearly twenty hours a day looking for vegetation to eat. They used their long curved tusks to dig through the snow to find plants and grasses to eat. Woolly mammoths lived to be nearly sixty years old.